This Little Tiger book

belongs to:

_____   _____

_____

_____   _____

For Jemima, happy finding-out time! x x ~ TC

For Isaac x ~ TW

LITTLE TIGER PRESS
1 The Coda Centre,
189 Munster Road, London SW6 6AW
www.littletiger.co.uk

First published in Great Britain 2014
This edition published 2014
Text copyright © Tracey Corderoy 2014
Illustrations copyright © Tim Warnes 2014
Visit Tim Warnes at www.ChapmanandWarnes.com
Tracey Corderoy and Tim Warnes have asserted their rights
to be identified as the author and illustrator of this work
under the Copyright, Designs and Patents Act, 1988
A CIP catalogue record for this book is available from the British Library

ISBN 978-1-84895-894-4
LTP/1400/0888/0314
Printed in China
2 4 6 8 10 9 7 5 3 1

Why?

Tracey Corderoy

Tim Warnes

LITTLE TIGER PRESS
London

Archie was a rhino with a
LOT of questions.

Sometimes, when he was finding answers,
Archie made a little bit of mess ...

And sometimes Archie made a LOT of mess!

Why do dropped things go SMASH?

Archie! Why don't you go and find Dad?

But wherever Archie went . . .

...his questions went too.

Why is mud so sticky, Dad?

Why are these roots so long?

ARRGH!

Mum, **Why** do spiders have so many legs?

Archie's parents decided that a rhino with a **LOT** of questions might like a trip to the museum.

Come on, Archie!

The museum was amazing.
There was SO much to see!

Archie had more questions than ever.

Why is the moon like a giant ball?

Why do spacemen float?

Why are little stars so bright and twinkly?

Some of these questions were **easy** to answer...

PRESS HERE to hear me ROAR!

Tricera

Mum, **Why** aren't there any dinosaurs NOW?

...but others were a **little** more tricky.

Archie loved the museum. There were buttons – and knobs – and things which bleeped, buzzed and twanged!

Off he went –
here, there and
everywhere...

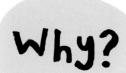

MANY wonderful whys later, there was still SO much to find out.

"Dad," said Archie, now quite sleepy, "why do ...

robots ...

go ..."

YAWN!

Suddenly, all of Archie's questions stopped.

Archie was quiet **all** the way home.

And he didn't say a
word through teatime ...   OR bath time.

As they turned out his light, Mum and Dad wondered if Archie had run out of questions **completely.**

But why **EVER** would they think that?

Inquisitive tots will love these great books from Little Tiger Press

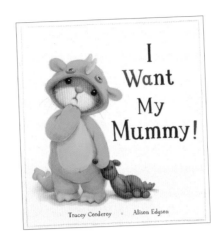

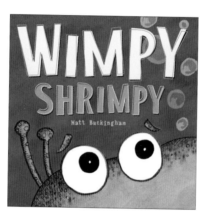

Oooo!

For information regarding any of the above titles
or for our catalogue, please contact us:
Little Tiger Press, 1 The Coda Centre,
189 Munster Road, London SW6 6AW
Tel: 020 7385 6333 • Fax: 020 7385 7333
E-mail: contact@littletiger.co.uk • www.littletiger.co.uk